C0-DUN-718

Treasure Hunt in the City

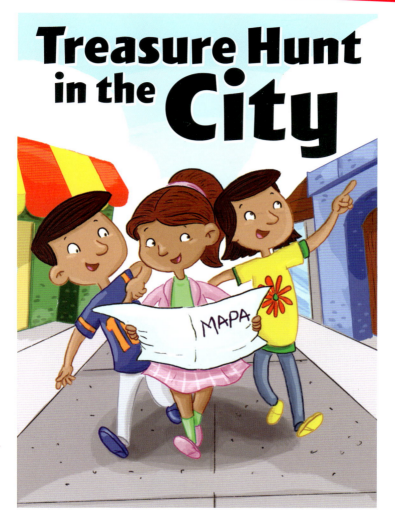

By Cynthia Harmony, M.A.
Illustrated by Brian Martin

Consultant
Chrissy Johnson, M.Ed.
Second Grade Teacher
Cedar Point Elementary School, Virginia

Publishing Credits
Rachelle Cracchiolo, M.S.Ed., *Publisher*
Emily R. Smith, M.A.Ed., *VP of Content Development*
Véronique Bos, *Creative Director*
Dani Neiley, *Associate Editor*
Kevin Pham, *Graphic Designer*

Image Credits
Illustrated by Brian Martin

Library of Congress Cataloging-in-Publication Data
Names: Harmony, Cynthia, author. | Martin, Brian (Brian Michael), 1978-
 illustrator.
Title: Treasure hunt in the city / by Cynthia Harmony, M.A. ; illustrated
 by Brian Martin.
Description: Huntington Beach, CA : Teacher Created Materials, [2022] |
 Audience: Grades 2-3. | Summary: "Ramona goes on her first big trip to
 Mexico City! She has to find a way to have fun with her cousins. Can she
 save her dream of becoming a successful world traveler?"-- Provided by
 publisher.
Identifiers: LCCN 2022003375 (print) | LCCN 2022003376 (ebook) | ISBN
 9781087605272 (paperback) | ISBN 9781087632131 (ebook)
Subjects: LCSH: Readers (Primary) | LCGFT: Readers (Publications)

5482 Argosy Avenue
Huntington Beach, CA 92649
www.tcmpub.com
ISBN 978-1-0876-0527-2

© 2023 Teacher Created Materials, Inc.
Printed in Malaysia.THU001.50393
This book may not be reproduced or distributed in any way without prior written consent from the publisher.

Table of Contents

Chapter One

Set for the Jet

Ramona pulled out her yellow suitcase from her closet. Dad was planning a work trip to Mexico City. She wanted to join him. This was her chance to be a world traveler!

"You're too young," said Dad.

"I just turned eight. My cousins are eight, too. It's a sign," insisted Ramona.

"Honey, it'll be hard because you don't speak Spanish," Dad explained.

"The kids will find ways to play," Mom reassured Dad.

Dad looked up from his computer and nodded.

Hooray!

Ramona had no siblings, so she loved the idea of playing with her twin cousins. And she could hardly wait to see Mexico.

Ramona called her best friend Kai for help. She needed his help to cram her suitcase shut.

"Wait! One last thing," said Ramona, adding a sparkly hat.

"I'd only bring my bike," giggled Kai.

Ramona laughed hard. "We're flying there, Kai!" she said. "Mexico City is one of the biggest cities in the world. It's far away and probably fancy. I'll share all my stories when I come back. And maybe I'll buy you a toy."

"Or Mexican candy," suggested Kai.

"And a postcard, like in the movies," promised Ramona.

She and Kai said goodbye by doing their secret handshake. Ramona gave Mom a hug as they left the house. She was ready to begin her adventure.

Chapter Two

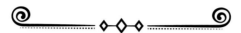

¡Hola, México!

On the flight, Ramona sank deep in her seat. She sighed and tried not to fidget. She was starting to feel bored on the long plane ride.

"*Agua*," said Dad. He pointed to his water cup.

"*Agua*," repeated Ramona.

She was going to learn so many Spanish words, like a true world traveler!

"Is the city fancy and exciting?" asked Ramona.

"You bet. It even has a castle," said Dad.

"Whoa!" exclaimed Ramona.

As the plane approached the city, Ramona looked out the window. The sun was setting over the city.

The lights were turning on. The twinkling city seemed to go on forever.

"There it is, *el Castillo* with the flag on top," Dad said, pointing.

"*El Castillo!*" Ramona squealed.

When they got to Dad's sister's house, Tía Gloria opened the door.

"*¡Hola!*" Ramona greeted them proudly.

The twins, Ana and Pablo, showered her with hugs and smiles. The house smelled so good. Spicy chicken, red rice, and beans awaited them. Ramona also tasted flan for the first time. It was a sweet and creamy dessert. She loved it!

"*¡Gracias!*" said Ramona.

It was the end of a long day. More fun would have to wait until tomorrow.

"Good night," she told everyone.

"*Buenas noches*, Ramona," said the rest of the family.

14

Early the next morning, Dad was off to work, and Ramona was ready to explore. The three cousins walked past cafés and tall buildings. There were so many new sounds and things to see. Lines of cars and elegant people rushed to work. Ramona fit right in with her glasses and her scarf.

"This is incredible!" she said, looking around in wonder. Her cousins smiled at her.

But there was a big problem in the big city.

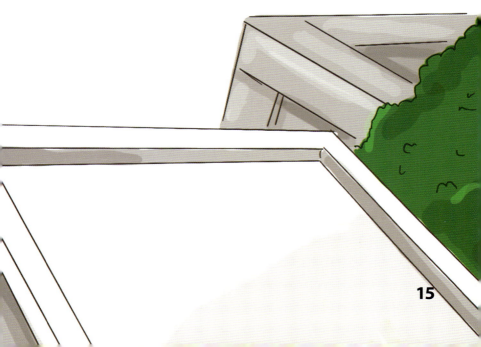

Chapter Three

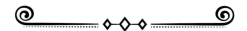

Say What?

Ramona asked to go to the left, but her cousins went to the right. When Dad wasn't there, they could not understand one another. She soon found out that she needed more than a few Spanish words.

Back at her cousins' house, Ramona asked Ana and Pablo to play. She talked slowly, pointed, and signaled with her hands a lot. But they didn't understand how to play the game. This was going to be harder than she'd thought.

Then, she noticed her cousins' school supplies and books. Maybe they had an English class!

17

She flipped through their books until she saw something she recognized. She picked up a book with the Eiffel Tower on the cover. Ramona's eyes opened wide. They were learning another language: French!

They know two languages! How cool is that? Too bad I don't know French, thought Ramona.

She thought writing Kai a note would make her feel better. But she missed him even more afterward.

Ramona felt lost. How could she feel lonely in a city with millions of people? This trip was her first big adventure and a dream come true. She couldn't give up now.

No sightseeing and no fun? No way! She was not putting away her fancy sunglasses and scarf. She would find a way to enjoy this trip.

Chapter Four

Treasure Hunt

How do world travelers find their way? Ramona wondered. In school, she learned that explorers used paper maps and stars to guide them.

That's it! she thought. She would make a map to find fun. But she didn't need stars or city lights. Ramona needed her family.

She motioned for Ana and Pablo to gather close. Then, she took out paper and colored pencils. Ramona wrote the word *candy* and drew it on the paper. Then, she drew a few other things to find, including Kai's gift.

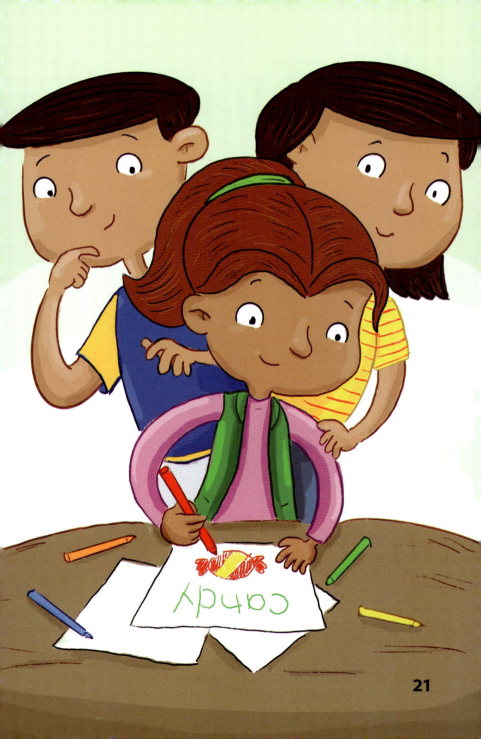

toy
juguete

swings
columpios

candy
dulces

slide
resbaladilla

paintings
pinturas

pastry
pan dulce

postcard
tarjeta postal

flowers
flores

Tía Gloria helped by telling them the Spanish word for each item. Then, Pablo wrote the words on the papers. Ana finished by taping the pictures together to make a big map! She wrote *mapa* on the back of it.

Place by place, step by step, the map made everyone stick close together. The cousins now understood where they were going. The treasure hunt was set to begin!

First, they found flowers at the castle gardens. When Tía Gloria stopped at a newsstand, the twins helped buy a postcard for Kai. At the art museum, Ramona saw a painting made by one of her favorite artists. At the children's museum, they spent most of their time giggling and going down the slide. In the gift shop, Ramona found a spinning toy for Kai. The next stop was a bakery. It sold tasty pastries.

Then, they passed stores with bright, fancy clothes to find the swings at the park by Tía Gloria's house. And they found a lot of Mexican candy to choose from at the marketplace.

Her cousins did not use the same words, but they shared the same smiles.

By the time they got home, they had found all their treasures.

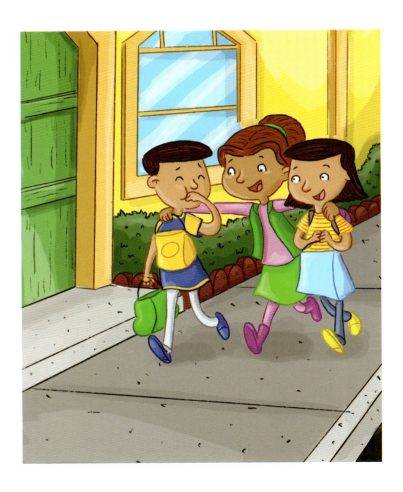

Chapter Five

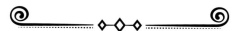

Hasta Luego Dance

Before long, Dad came back from work. Ramona told him all about her adventures.

"That's amazing, Ramona," he said. "You found a way to create fun for everyone!"

Soon, Ramona and her dad had to catch a plane home. Ramona packed slowly. She imagined telling Kai about her adventures and teaching him some Spanish words. She grinned.

Then, she thought about saying goodbye to her Mexican family. She frowned.

Being a world traveler was not easy. Ramona came out of the room with her bags.

"*Una sorpresa*…for you," said Ana.

Pablo turned on some music. A happy tune and colorful lights filled the room.

"I love surprises and dance parties!" exclaimed Ramona.

They shimmied.

They boogied.

They laughed.

Everyone moved to the same rhythm.

"*Hasta luego*," said the twins.

"It means 'see you later,'" said Dad.

After one last group hug, Ramona was certain she would see them again. Her days as a world traveler had just begun. Maybe they could all travel to France together one day.

"*Hasta luego*," she said, waving from the cab window. Ramona smiled. She couldn't wait for her next adventure!

About Us

The Author
Cynthia Harmony was born in Mexico City. She learned English as a kid. And she knows a bit of French, too. She loves art, writing children's books, and traveling. She has visited 15 countries so far.

The Illustrator
Brian Martin is an author and illustrator from Richmond, Virginia. As an illustrator, Martin loves to tell stories with his bright and whimsical art and has illustrated over 30 children's books. Martin is always looking for opportunities to bring stories to life for both children and adults to enjoy. When he isn't busy writing and making art, Martin loves playing with his four amazing kids.